10 Scary Monsters

P3,
Scoil Chiaráin,
Dublin

THE O'BRIEN PRESS
DUBLIN

First published 2007 by The O'Brien Press Ltd,
12 Terenure Road East, Rathgar, Dublin 6, Ireland.
Tel: +353 1 4923333; Fax: +353 1 4922777
E-mail: books@obrien.ie
Website: www.obrien.ie

ISBN: 978-1-84717-002-6

British Library Cataloguing-in-Publication Data
10 scary monsters
1. Monsters - Juvenile fiction 2. Counting - Juvenile fiction 3. Children's stories
I. Murphy, Kay II. Scoil Chiarain (Clara, Ireland) III. Ten scary monsters
823.9'2[J]

1 2 3 4 5 6 7 8 9 10
07 08 09 10 11 12

The O'Brien Press receives assistance from

Cover illustration: Francesca Carabelli

Editing, typesetting, layout, design:
The O'Brien Press Ltd
Printing: KHL, Singapore

10 Ten scary monsters came knocking at my door

One scary monster
fell through the floor!

9

Nine scary monsters
got dressed for bed

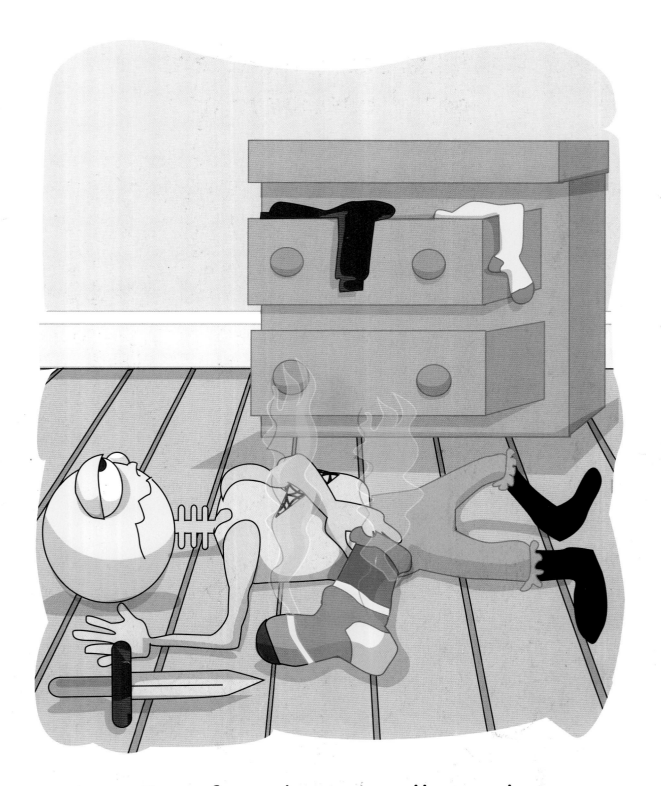

One found my smelly sock
and fell down dead!

Eight scary monsters in my bed at night

One saw his shadow
and ran off in fright

7

Seven scary monsters
eating green jelly

One went to hospital with a
pain in his belly

Six scary monsters followed me to school

One became a teacher
'Cos we thought he was cool

5 Five scary monsters in a hot air balloon

One got left behind,
now he lives on the moon

Four scary monsters
fishing by the sea shore

One was caught by a shark
and was seen no more

3 Three scary monsters singing in the rain

One was too skinny
and he fell down a drain

2 Two scary monsters went to the zoo

One fell into the elephant poo!

1 One scary monster left all alone

She wasn't scary...

- So I brought her home!

The End

1 Monster, 2 Monsters, 3 Monsters, 4 ...

Whose Monster?

Seán Brennan

Jordan Robinson

Meghann Coules

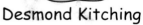

Desmond Kitching

Anthony Horgan

Kirstie Caffrey

Danielle Bird

Darren Higgins

Carla Duffy

Niamh Ryan